Dewey Doe

By Cody Adam

Dorrance Publishing Co
585 Alpha Drive
Suite 103
Pittsburgh, PA 15238
Visit our website at *www.dorrancebookstore.com*

ISBN: 979-8-88729-257-1
EISBN: 979-8-88729-757-6

The children of Lucifer do not like to be used in any act. They told me by their confession of existing to me in being able to be dead gone, not used. Yet my ability, they tell me with agreement in being loyal to me by showing me what they've been doing, living as a cry towards me. I help them with allowance by God. The children live as one tide to Lucifer's tail. Meeting in my time of life assume one has a beholder of this entity Lucifer the humanity destruction format in paranormal state of being. The ability I have is to kill Lucifer and help the ones that need help. I tend to do that in my lifetime spent. This act grabbing $400,000 with the made of the money is worth than the money labeled itself, is key factor for the locals in need as it is my pleasure to help them and have them not to bump into us and push us around in life with it being a free dose of happiness for the ones who are going to receive the money as I do this with you my life mission," Dewey tells his elected right-handed man, his best friend, Tim Kelly, a skinny muscle tone mixed white man with African roots only in his hair and having green eyes.

Dewey and Tim are in a white 1999 Camaro parked across the street from a steel-made warehouse. Parked in a neighboring warehouse lot that makes vitamins, anything healthy in food to support the company Strength Peacan. Tim got a job working there knowing the warehouse next to it makes money, its federally owned. "A four-man group, you get the uniforms and watch them. The way they act, the walk, the chat as they're doing their job, watch them, everything, the convo, gestures while they're walking. Is it formal? Any worries? You mention it to me. Like I said, the ability is prayer muscle works into an act or acts. The muscle I am developing with you. The night before we act on this, I pray with you, and you do your 3'6'9's in Jesus Christ, amen exercise in breathing motion." Dewey speaks more to his friend, his only trusted peer in life since they met in childhood. He speaks with intention; he is passing knowledge to Tim from his knowing so his peer will be able to use the ability for the rest of his natural-born life. Dewey sticks a toothpick in his mouth, mint flavored.

"Uniforms, house IDs, and bag of clothes for quick change," Tim responded.

"Yeah, that's right. We move when there's a small shift change at midnight. There will be four security guards and three crew leaders going in as we go out. We get there at nine, our way in with the IDs, four will be at work working to get inside where the money is and will do. We come at 11:55 a.m. with the van as the four boxes will be ready to load up with the crew walking out as that shift change at twelve," Dewey explained.

The two are in the car bought by Dewey with his ability came in full worked; able and intact to do acts in a magic sighting manner as is a mystical act. He cashed out a new atm machine called cash station, by having a child of Lucifer confess its nature and its form by having the dollar bills dispense out of the machine nonstop until it's ran out of the bills. The line he said to make it possible was "Confess you are used for this design of currency now in the king's name Jesus Christ amen!" All the money soon came out of the cash station machine, and the year was 1996, Now its 2013 and Dewey enjoys his 1999 white Camaro. Dewey did other acts as well, in 2001 he befriended a prostitute and healed her of AIDS by her eating his cum daily.

Dewey worked out hard during these times in pressure having his muscle form underneath his fattening. He had the offspring confess its ability to heal the lady from AIDS as its part of its nature is to form to make AIDS as it makes sickness upon humanity. Dewey also healed sixty men of colon cancer by making his own tea plants. He grew tea plants during his forties and had the plants tide in the power of the offspring being in confession mode unlock the plant's ability to heal the cancer in the colon when consumed. Dewey prayed upon the soil and the seed and they made of it getting touched by the sun, the heat to grow and the eating of the water from its roots. Dewey prayed upon that act ability having a showing of the leaves being greener and solid in the look. Dewey comes to his consciousness of wisdom with God in figuring out these remedies to help another with his mystic ability. This act he is doing with Tim is a bigger act. It involves stealing against the federal and it's his first act like this.

It's the night before the act to go in the federal warehouse and steal the money. Dewey and Tim are at an enriched famed hotel room in Delaware state. "Dear entity of I the ownership as God as he is God meaning you the entity that heals me and directs me, I pray the stable of this act be cleansed in the reason of doing so, to give the needy the money worth to survive and get out of any poor rut they are in, I pray for the smooth walk of this as walking to a car, as walking to you, God, by afar and getting close to you, my entity, I pray in Jesus Christ's name amen."

Dewey prays with Tim in the night at a hotel room in Delaware state. Dewey and Tim unclose their hands. Dewey thinks of the needy, the know of needing something to eat and not have the thing to give you to get the food. Dewey has been in a homeless area once and knows why the rent and the natural bills need to be paid.

Dewey speaks to Tim. "This goes well. The ability I have

will show itself in awe and you decide whether or not to continue with me, friend. Three motions for three parts as a whole the flesh, soul, and spirit are made. Six motions of full circle all life creation comes full circle in our life form made. And nine motions for our God being our armor, our light the know of the universe, our God the weaponry against wrong and evil in being our consciousness, the nine in Jesus Christ's name amen," Dewey says while he works out an exercise doing crunches on the bed.

"Right Dewey, this act goes well, I bet. I still decide, Dewey, to go further in what you do with your 3'6'9' in Jesus Christ, amen. Yeah, I like the workout and been here still with you Dewey. It's stealing against the evil power, no worries in humanity laws, Dewey. It's Robin Hood at its finest.," Tim says back at Dewey, getting into doing an exercise, grabbing his yellow strength rope.

"You say yes, confessing it is ability to do, I will teach you, it can be an ease in life with the Lord, my friend," Dewey responds back to Tim. They work out before they go to sleep.

It's the next night in summer of 2014 in the neighborhood of warehouses in the outskirts of a city of Delaware state. The weather is calm, summer-heated air.

"The cameras are blurred. We've got forty-five minutes, boss. Uniforms on, tag on, and the wait for the black van is on; walking to the room. It's 10:38 p.m.," Icy says to Dewey on the 2009 military-issued walkie-talkie fitted in Icy's right ear. Icy is walking six foot three with light brown hair, full white male, a side worker for the mafia, going to the room where the money is.

"Look at the labeled. It will be worded $100,000 with red marking and the count will be as a1a2a3a4 and the equipoise of the four boxes is 214.5 pounds," Dewey said. Dewey knowing the boxes' looks by seeing them in a vision during his sleep for the past two years by the offspring of Lucifer. Icy confirms what Dewey said by tapping his walkie-talkie, making a snapping sound. While they are walking, Icy tells his third man to stay around the lunch area, having a doorway to it from the aisle for look out. The third man steps into the lunch area, fills in act like he is on lunch break, while the fourth man waits around the east side exit area—not having security bars and not having a security guard—being a lookout and just in case a path is closed, he will be the one to clear a path for them to exit.

Icy walks with his second man with a blue steeled cart on eight wheels in the white based color aisle with blue walls. He mentions to Dewey he is close to the room. "When you get inside the room, it will have a glass sliding door with a touchscreen passcode, left top to right connect the three dots and you are in," Dewey said. Icy confirms what Dewey said by tapping again on his walkie-talkie. Icy walks more, comes to the dark-blue-colored door to the room and swipes his ID badge to enter the room. Icy pushes the dark-blue cart in the room, coming to a glass door. Icy then connects the three dots that are in rows of three with nine dots altogether from left to right on the top as Dewey explained. The glass sliding door opens and Icy's second man pushes the blue steel cart having a baby blue plastic covering on the singled bar of the cart.

"Need to hurry, bro. The blur says we got forty-five minutes. I say we only have fifteen minutes. Soon we get out of this room, we jog little to the exit, agreed?"

"Yes, in the manner of walked smoothed, I like this," Icy responds to his coworker. Icy sees the money in the steel boxes shelved as the library shelfs of books having labels matching the worth and the year on the rows of the shelves. Icy looks and looks with finally confirming four boxes that match Dewey's description in the right, back of the room. Icy and his man load up the cart with the 55-pound boxes. Icy leaves the room and is now walking back on the white aisle with his coworker in extreme excitement, having his heartbeat in a fast pace being controlled, being happy knowing how smooth this act is going. Dewey makes a breaking sound while chewing on a mint flavored toothpick having the motion of the chew with his ability being the act to have the stability of stealing the money go without touch.

"I got the money on the cart; going to the exit; it's 11:34 p.m.," Icy responds to Dewey walking past the lunchroom in the long 145-foot hallway aisle in the steel diamond glass warehouse. The third man sees that the two are jogging, so he continues the pattern and jogs too. They reach to the end of the hallway, coming to a big space having the east side exit in this huge eighty-square-foot space, passing men and woman who works there. The fourth man sees them and swipes his ID badge on the pad connecting to the door and opens the door. Dewey sees the door open of the warehouse as he is in the black van. Tim opens the side door as Dewey strolls closer to the east side door parking five feet in front of the door having the side door face the east exit door of the warehouse with the camera still blurred.

Only a few security guards have been walking out of lane to watch out for something from seeing the camera's blur. The four men grab a box and carry the boxes to the black van, passing the exit in a sweet motion as a wide receiver passes the guard man to get open. The four men put the boxes in the black van and see the four security guards and the three crew leaders at the south end entrance coming in as they get inside the black van and Icy pushes a button on the laptop in the van that gets the cameras to not to do another blur vision in thirty minutes, also ending the software connection from the laptop to the security cameras.

Dewey is in the driver seat when he looks back seeing that act is done. Dewey then leaves from being parked and takes a right on the street coming out the entranceway from the steel-made warehouse in the neighborhood filled with warehouses. He drives out of the neighborhood going to his Camaro to load the money in his car with his crew having their share as well.

"This evening, the outcome of the riot case, the ability to take vitamins as eating a hamburger, and the mystic wonder of the money mail out of thin air, having a letter sent to the police all this evening at four. Evil of these times, as decades of last century together, is enemy for life with I bested to show truth and the will of our Lord," Dewey says as he sees the TV screen of the new millennium century made as he wears a do-rag sitting in a loaf black leather eased back comfort chair in his rented apartment home.

No one is counting the acts of Dewey and the law making him a criminal in what he does in healing another. Locals received money that its ten-times worth than it says: five-dollar bill worth fifty dollars and so on. Giving money to the locals is just one of his acts in the muscle he forms growing up in an abused childhood, being left alone, smacked by his father, and raped by his mother, being cast out, left alone more after having two siblings a little brother and a little sister. Having not known it happens to his two siblings and not knowing not to do the simple act towards another in true purpose and reason to do so. Dewey learned you touch me wrong; I touch you wrong back. Dewey would intend to abuse back and once raped back growing up and he has not done it again when it went to the courts of the reality.

At the age of eight, Dewey shot his mother in the head.

His mother would rape him and bested to kept him lonely. Every time Dewey tried to get friends, his mother would barge in and take over, keeping Dewey away from his friends. Tim was the only one kept to him by knowing what happens to him. He went to the courts, and it ruled that his little brother was playing with the gun and killed her. The father lost custody of his little brother and sister, their father was not charged. He owns the gun in legal terms. The father would abuse him often, put Dewey in closed throat grasping for air hands lock, getting Dewey close to the point of death and release him. Dewey's father blames his wife Dewey's mother on how she died, yet he would abuse Dewey having a crazy trait: no realization he is doing wrong to Dewey.

Having this done to Dewey, the abuse, it unfolds the act of supernatural made, making Dewey a mutant of some sort, having himself know what he is able to do. He hears a whisper defined in the government that hearing voices is psycho be labeled schizophrenia. He made the entity of the paranormal show itself to be his determination to find what is happening to him. The whisper became self-showing in doing acts from Dewey's emotions by having a neighbor feel sorry for him and help him leave his father. At the age of sixteen, when Dewey was going to the courts, the neighbor went to a mafia boss on Dewey's father and warned him that if he abuses Dewey again, the boss will have him killed in a painful way. Dewey's father stopped for a while. Being close to death many times from his daddy. His father would bring him back alive making sure he would have the ability to breathe as he releases his chokehold grasp. He did so in a routine manner. One time Dewey never knew of his blind spot until his dad hit him hard enough from the back of his head where Dewey blacked out, awake with trouble breathing until his dad comforted him of the motion that helps him breathe by rubbing his head in a relaxing manner and his upper muscles.

His dad knew at this comfort Dewey tends to collect his breath naturally. He did the act again when Dewey got probation off a sexual abuse case towards a lady that has the same personality as his mom. Dewey couldn't prove she was raping him, and the story proves Dewey was the evildoer. Dewey kissed back knowing this lady was not his blood mother. Dewey again found in the same situation as his mother would do him, she would not allow Dewey go back home unless he does sexual acts with her when Dewey came to her house to visit her in having help in schooling. Once Dewey told her no and stop she pressed charges against Dewey. Dewey was found guilty of all charges. First case makes him have probation, otherwise Dewey would go to prison for five years.

When Dewey came home from the sentencing, Dewey's dad's temper rushed to his brain, and he began to abuse Dewey, grabbing his neck, tightening his hands so Dewey will not be able to breathe. Suddenly his dad began coughing and dropped down to the ground, dead with no ability of slow breathing to death. Again, at his age sixteen, he learned prayer was the outcome of learning his ability. Anything he thought of the outcome went to God in life. Every answer to a question that came to his mind about his ability of clinching his face, staring hard at a thought or word and the thought happens nor the word appears on TV or in the papers he would read in an instant when he thinks of it. All learned stable humanity feelings came from teachings about God. He was staring at a prayer that weaponized evil to be dead as his dad was abusing him knowledgeable how his dad was right to punish him.

No weapon from evil shall prosper against me and he was thinking the evil be the foot stole to be gone dead no living another day to hurt me. He stared at his dad a long time, 5'10" black haired, chubby fattening around his muscles popping out naturally and giggles for the first time after his dad dropped down dead, knowing God killed his dad for him. That's when it's clear to Dewey it is God's gift for him, this bearable paranormal act against him hearing a whisper that sounds like a growl at times from his abuse taken from both of his parents and the need to say it is not real at times having him see hallucinations to have given direction towards God when he questions the experience and be with, he: God. Dewey rests his eyes watching the TV show, seeing the money being given to the locals in the mailbox and have the buzz surrounding what he did be on the news gives him reassurance on his guided mission.

September 23, 2014

"The seating, find your comfort spot. Feel the satisfaction of the comfort, see, think of a prayer in need, yet be a want in sight of knowing. Court, the wooden area, smell the carpet. See the act that got you here, even you commit a crime or be there suing someone. Breathe in, by the time you crack the ability by breathing the simple form of living. You win every case by just breathing in the ability enhancing yourself to another mode while one would not recognize. I picked the outcome by thought in breath in 70/30 case when we are the 30, we will win by the grace of our acts in everyday routine we will win in breath of he the Lord. Stable words in the end of breathing on winning a case.

"Simple exercise in talk uncracking the ability for us in living a better life; 3'6'9' in Jesus Christ amen is that in body moving exercise goes with power breathing." Dewey explains, giggling and talking to Tim. "Once you tap the ability of your own pattern in life as Jesus Christ be king, he be king in what you do, courts anything would be a breeze," Dewey continues. "Best not be in the courts in criminal in the long end run. Just one smack in need of the criminal human that are shameful evil out there, at the time of life living it need stable from the awe of the ability you are receiving and have; be sure to be smooth, the stable at play at all times, use sleep for the rest, while awake work on awareness at the foremost."

Dewey describes more of the ability he has by prayer define. "Drink coffee nor the routine drink you like, now days more of it mainstream has healthy picks, even coffee. Mind your thought in the name of Jesus Christ at all times as usual stress of the positive feeling in life, Satisfaction adrenaline rush in life, think the thought *in Jesus Christ's name amen* at all times during those, even with the drink you pick, more holy healthier swallows." Dewey speaks more of the ability describing a way as he looks at the menu of the restaurant him and Tim are at. A lawyer just sits on the left next to Tim holding just a laptop with its leather case. The five-foot-nine lawyer with black hair and brown beard says hi to Dewey and Tim.

"Well, everything is going smoothly. We will keep going smoothly as I see it, came from a chat from the judge. The deal is in, accepted. You will own the business, and the load sum 150 million more that the state is offering, the case is at that. Best luck to you, Dewey. This case can't happen again." The lawyer shakes hands with Dewey and leaves the table and the restaurant located in downtown New York City. Where Richard Green's establishment is at New York City, the guy Dewey sued for hiring minors for porn, they were seventeen at the time.

"You mean to tell me, by prayer from God the almighty

gave you that. The business and 150 million. Dewey, what is the meaning, long shot getting that proved to judge that they were minors to unlock more what that dude was doing. Hail Mary, Dewey. That dude was feeding a lot of people, the showdown of this!" Tim alerted as Dewey orders a soda pop and baked fish.

"Dude, the core purpose is knowing. Reason the know of its define, the government denies God in the place where he is worship money, the government is the people. Richard Green denies God in feeding those people, not in church, but the money, the courts and civil life is exact government. He denies getting there to a paradise still living afterwards," Dewey assures Tim's awe more as Tim orders the same baked fish and a soda pop. Dewey is wearing a cross a preacher gave him. With the amount of money that kept him stable, he bought upgrades to the necklace. He has a jeweler in New Jersey City that enjoys working on his cross. Making it all diamond is Dewey's goal for the necklace.

He met the preacher on the south side of the city. Baptism was the chat lingo. Dewey enjoyed learning about baptism. Known later after Dewey got baptize at the age of twenty-four, is the grace of the connection to God and the works of the acts of God by being close to him in living life stable within the government structure way of life. Dewey giggles at the knowledge of grace in his life.

Tim's cell phone starts to ring as he is still seated in the restaurant with Dewey, the silver 2012-made phone with a pencil stick rings a hip-hop rhythm. Tim pushes Call. "Hello."

"Tell the boss, checking in. Everything good, on standby ready for the next move."

"Okay, be by the phone for the next order," Tim responds as he ends the call.

"How is the cell?" Dewey asks Tim after he noticed him

taking the call. "The phone should last long. The battery is up there in best standard."

"The phone is neat. Been writing down what you told me in my phone. What's the next act, man?" Tim asks Dewey, being reminded he is doing what Dewey told him to do, noticing his words and beginning to see headaches as a hallucination with the ability in being stable passing through the headache without stress and feeling strengthened more as he has Dewey's words mentally help him at times when he gets low and tired out nor pressured out in unable to do the motion or the act itself in making a mystic ability as Dewey's been explaining to Tim.

"The men are there?" Tim nods yes. "Have them get a month stay. We're going to scope out the state of Missouri. Intel is Richard Green lives there. Going to need them four to have a stable job for a story, just one. We're going to check in a casino hotel in Saint Louis, going to send them four an hour away for days and months looking for this guy, and I'm going to show you more of my ability in the casino games. I have been sensing you more by the minute and it has me thinking you've been uncracking, passing through the harden to achieve an ability of mystic power; glow in a different way being transformed as in the new testament the king Jesus Christ transformation act and acts with study more of the word of the Lord.

"The question, friend, is what to do for our local? My drive is ending an evil rutted routine, many as I can, friend. Our reason is our local, our purpose is our foundation, answer that question when unlocked, life will be busy in an unstressed manner when the shocking of the outcome of the ability is there. Richard Green happens to be another one." Dewey chats about the next act in having a question be thoughted to answer in being the main simple plan of the act with him focusing on his friend Tim Kelly being unlocked in sight of see by prayer in receiving an ability for the common good, self-checked.

"When the food comes is the reminder of the evil acts here in life, eat consume the food digest its end, use its form for the benefit of evil not having a route to live by shitting it out to soil. Slaying Lucifer faster in time now with going after Richard Green. He has not found any sense of human in him. Two dudes sitting by the bar completeness shy ignoring that I caught them eyeing we. After we eat, we leave the city by plane. Keep the car here grab a taxi and head to the airport. My know to you confirm yet again the Lucifer I speak about how one been trailing me for it don't know how badly the offspring of its user Lucifer has cast outed itself, kept living by my force and has old ancient memories with tomahawks: the Indians. As said before reminding you to have a stable muscle enough adrenaline energy as about to always play a real game or a match in Jesus Christ amen."

Dewey talks more about having a plan to leave in notice from a stranger eye lurking on sense of true paranoia in basis reality to act on it by his consciousness; his experiences in the past of one knowing about him. As he was thirty-three years old, he killed a cop without going to prison nor going to the courts. Dewey found out this six-foot-tall police officer was doing wrong; he was abusing women who sold their bodies. He would have them do sexual acts for them to get out of jail term. Dewey found a way to have a stand-up confrontation with him for him to squeeze his fist after squeezing every muscle in his body to cause the cop to have a heart attack. Everyone around him confirmed Dewey did nothing but had an argument with him without foul play.

After it was done, a six foot two, long, black-haired dark

skin Indian man fronted Dewey, called him a rebel fat boy saying only he knows what Dewey did with a message coming from his leader giving Dewey a worry. All Dewey did was pray more and came to realization a force is not going to stand down in this war begun. The waiter sets the stand down on its four legs, putting the circle plate with their food on it being on the left side of the restaurant near the bar.

"Both baked fish, you look well romantically in your gear," Tim said in happiness. She says thank you. Passing off Dewey's dish to him. She is wearing a black and red skirt to the knees and a white T-shirt having the restaurant's name Big Al house on the back. She wears it having more of the eye of lust from Tim. "What is your name?"

The waiter responds, "Kristen."

"Mine is Tim, nice to meet you."

"Nice to meet you too." She then walks away in the restaurant crowd passing the bar. Dewey in prayer hands before he eats, and Tim looks and begins to pray too.

"Where to?"

"To JFK airport. Anyways the key point finding the ideal local thought your drive for the common good with the ability is money straight on point thought, that is when again speak stable, healthy and wealthy in Jesus Christ amen. You will feel more empowered in everyday life. Sure, going to chill once at the casino and you will see Adam and Eve is always perfect in winning. as I will be winning games, my friend," Dewey says to his friend, Tim, in a white van taxi with purple coating seats. Tim is in awe as he is always since he trusted Dewey decades ago before they split in life and later found each other again. By then Dewey was equipped with his mystic ability. He has shown Tim and Tim trusted him ever since. Tim has bank in his bank account from Dewey and he is understanding the feeling of stopping evil with Dewey finding his heart reason while he lives with Dewey this way.

"Yeah, man. I'm excited. Just need to give a call to my girl, man," Tim responds back to Dewey. Dewey then thinks of Karen, then giggles while resting his head on the comfy purple head seat.

"Yes, I'd like to have two tickets on the next flight to Saint Louis, Missouri, please."

"Next flight is an hour wait."

"Yes, I'll take it."

"Okay, $437.69," the airport clerk tells Dewey the price of the flight. Dewey then gives the clerk a card to pay for it.

"Let's find a bar near the spot; we got an hour wait," Dewey said to Tim while holding the tickets just printed out for them with walking towards their gateway number. They been walking for five minutes in the airport going west.

"In luck, Dewey, one right near it. Let's go," Tim said to Dewey in excitement. Tim quickly walks in the tavern built inside the airport, having gold flashy entranceway wooden plaque for the name of the bar American pub. "Your house beer please?" Tim ordered beer for them both. They are sitting in the right corner near the wall by the entrance of the bar. "Stable, the word defines the high life with the Lord. A drinking problem is doing it all the time. The key is with the Lord on these substances in the fashion of a wonderful time. Always with the Lord." Dewey breaks a chat mentioning what he enjoys in life is the Lord in everything he does, even brushing his teeth. The beers then arrive by a male worker.

"A problem is when it's noticed, bro," Tim replies in being in quick motion to drink his drink.

"It with negative or I call evil thoughts and expect a stable outcome with drinking all the time in having personality develop in being a low-life, with prayer with the Lord, characteristics and personality be cleaner with rightful agreements with knowing the Lord as the entity he has shown in my life." Dewey then giggles drinking his beer. "Now he has shown in your life with your trust, stable money, no worries and great deal of potential in sexual mating game," Dewey says enjoying his frosted beer.

"Yes, I'm enjoying it, Dewey. The unlocking, the ability you keep saying. I feel more energy, more focused feeling, and more aware of alertness. I am best to be able to move a person like you do, interacting with another, my best to find the reason would be a set of keys, bro! Have it confessed and show it sorriest in given benefit to I and given it the advantage for another in the common good living life bro, as you said." Tim chats more explaining his side of unlocking finally admitting to Dewey what he has experienced with enjoying his drink as well. They both have more time left, so they order more beers.

"I see we write out applications in Saint Louis where we headed until one of us is hired. Basic jobs, bars are a delight on this one. Just one flaw for both of us, we got priors and a stamp on our background. Best to lee-way grab a job anyway at that company if need to go to the bar." Dewey cell phone then rings, "Hello, Dewey, this is Brad."

"Yeah, hello, sir."

"Good news. The cards are good to go, and $50,000 is being deposited in your bank account given now, and a card going to the address given on file will be the card to use for free bus rides in the city and where at use, they will be two of them for you, Dewey."

"Great, Brad, glad to hear the case is settled."

"Nice working with you. Goodbye, Dewey." A street lawyer from the mafia was on the other end of the call. Dewey met him in 2002 after meeting big shot white collar corrupts and the blue-collar high-class toxics. The lawyer is good beneath the table settlements having violence define its weight if no agreement is made. "Good news, money is set now as we go. Order another one; then we split," Dewey said to Tim, having a thirst for beer.

The tobacco Dewey is smoking is his favorite blend of regular tobacco from his home city, English .9 is the name of the blend of the house blend selective of Charlie Tobacco his favorite tobacco store. As he breathes out the tobacco, he channels his pain in the smoke and feels the smoke heighten in his lungs to express his satisfaction in smoking in front of the Lord, he's been smoking for forty years and is still able to run a trummil. He feels his pain in the tobacco, breathes, and sees himself as that rebel ending the evil routine of continuance without learned lesson as to be far gone people in the life they choose.

He sees their tears in the stable they showed from the act in all the people he saw in life, inhales the tobacco thinking hard about death in giving it to the lungs, he sees that act happening, making evil breathe to its needs to death to clean the smoking of the tobacco in he having no negative effects; to have virgins lungs sparkle in breathes at times as his routine in smoking praying in faith with the Lord in what he is doing the works to end the rutted poison of humanity. Dewey and Tim are at a famed casino hotel in Saint Louis. Dewey breathes smoke more sitting on the lofty chair that was next to this corner table in west of the room. He is sitting in relaxed comfort thinks of the death of his dad and begins to giggle. Tim notices and gets excited knowing every time Dewey giggles, he gets to completing acts that gets him to be richly stable as staying in this hotel for a month, checking in with not needing a job for money to pay for another month.

For Dewey in his realization of the giggling helps his overall wellness in his proper health with his ability not having a disease root nor wearing glasses, hearing aids, and having teeth problems, he just deals with the age root that overall, slowly in his decades of living. As he smokes more, he thinks of grabbing Icy's blood who is living at the hotel too with his three men. Dewey had Tim go to school to find out to take blood and the ways of the needle when they first got back together. Tim is stretching out doing stretches getting ready to sleep. Dewey prays, breathing the tobacco smoke symbol power of breath of the Lord as he breathes life in Adam's nostrils. Breathing more he smiles knowing the mafia wants nothing to do with Icy no more. How he doesn't learn to stay away from the dark net they told Dewey. Easy money to them is not that way.

Icy's blood's savory tease taste of Dewey's mouth knowing how tasty his blood will be in prayer giving him sickness, a plaque to enter heaven gates in return of the excess hurt he does in life in not learning to stop an evil behavior in being stable living life to do so. Dewey end his prayer form smoke that filled the room and sets to sleep having Richard Green and another young man on his mind to kill them for them doing illegal sex trade after he sued them. He giggles, knowing they live in Missouri, and he is there.

"I'm in Missouri, the keys of the apartment house are in the mailbox, everything runs. You can stay there as long as long as you like," Dewey said on his cell phone in the afternoon in the hotel room stacked with food having two refrigerators.

"Okay thanks, Dewey, I miss you and love you," Karen says on the other end of the call.

"I miss and love you too. I'm here in Missouri for a while and I will be back at that apartment after I'm done. If you're there, I will take care of you more. You are my number one boo," Dewey said in the manner being loved in the casino hotel filled with single fashion to mate.

"I trust you will be there soon; I'm leaving today heading over there, love to see you, Dewey. I like you being happy, Dewey, and you show it by being with me, I've seen it," Karen says as Dewey relaxes on the bed after eating hashbrowns and French toast from the cafeteria of the hotel diner his breakfast.

"Yeah, I can't hide it, or would hide who makes me happy. That's why I'm glad I contacted you and be able to help you. I got to do work this afternoon and definitely will do my best to hurry and see you. Call me if any need my love."

"Yes, Dewey, I will, I love you."

"Love you too." Dewey ends the call. "Got the blood, I need it to mix with apple vinegar," Dewey mentions to Tim. Tim gives him the tubes of blood. Minutes later....

Dewey begins to channel god in him more as he learned from going out of breath by his dad whom used to squeeze the life out of him numerous times. He remembers one time as he sees his dad's arms and shoulders feeling his hands squeezing his airway in his neck while radio music was on he was hearing loud sounds before the air grasp no more oxygen. The sound later turned into his giggles. By that he is able to hear himself giggling, which channels his self-wellness in perfect adrenaline rush to cherish his health in a comfort feel of living by the act of giggling. Dewey then speaks as his eyes are closed. "My dear father the unchanged life is the blood of the persons I'm going to drink. I pray in Jesus Christ's name death comes to them soon in known sick chain they support is the evil Lucifer the devil Satan that consumes Humanity to be evil sick to its rut in Jesus Christ's name amen. My father and I drink.

Dewey drinks the blood of four men that work for him in five years strong. Dewey has not seen, experienced, or had a sense of their life change from their evil rutted nature needing money for the spoils of the evil energy life here in this country United States of America: the unlearned from punishment. He drinks the four men's blood with apple cider vinegar with Tim as Tim learns how to draw blood for this act. Tim smiles with Dewey as they both are drinking the drink in a red plastic cup. Tim, being a second Adam, an elemental being to use to bring these men to death in plague upon themselves, after this act that involves another death with a payload only design for Tim and Dewey while a little sum of the money is being in the four men's face for the current stable of them being used.

Dewey sits back of the chair in the hotel room as Tim sits on the second bed near him, both having a high and being relaxed. Dewey consuming the effects of praying in that nature by a feeling of calmness in relaxed collected thoughted manner in purpose meaning breath. Breathing, having the feel of the air, the touch hits the lungs as pure virgin lungs within Dewey's every breath after this prayer having confirmed from God in that way sitting in the light black steel chair in full mode in being able: function to a structure living life with mystic supernatural ability.

Dewey opens his eyes seeing the high rich hotel room, smiles. He is set to do the plan and giggles knowing he is going to giggle later seeing God's act of love for him in the rebel heart in his growth to have the evil nature stopped by death, as it lives in humanity's waiting rooms with gnawing horns. Dewey sighs amen. He notices the money in his green bag with wheels and giggles. He gets out of the chair, grabs some money out of the bag, tells Tim he will be back, and walks out of the hotel room to give money to the needy of the night in Saint Louis.

Dewey has been awake for four hours. It's now 2:23 p.m. the next day. He is staring, watching TV. The high-priced cable channels are free, come with the style of the room, there are rooms with hot tubs inside and Dewey enjoys seeing the routine of the channels of the cable television. The repeat and the new rings of the commercials, the TV shows have the fad about the culture look they are about and the certain movies they play on cable. Dewey grins, knowing the only way to stop the junk is to enlighten the end of the routes and journey of the evil men and women that enjoy its wealth in life.

Dewey stares more at the TV sitting at the edge of his bed grinning, seeing the sight of a structure evil: a witch spell living a Lucifer offspring's play as the entertainment story matches the news in the form of what is next on TV. The news show partakes what has been in action TV shows having the mystery of the act, especially involving murder and that sense of nature. Dewey has been sighting this for years, seeing the news with the TV show entertainment growth to wild spree of crimes and drama to the extreme meeting the status quo the president later in the media. Dewey is at heart with this, more so by the response he receives from using his ability.

First a Native American man and later a group of black-haired women told Dewey, "What you see you can't stop." All five were dancing upon him in a teasing sensual motion said this as they were still friendly with Dewey at a high fancy club called Atlantis in Nevada while Dewey was thirty-eight years old. Dewey taken the hit hard by these strangers having a clue about Dewey. He manifested with lemon juice having the women's blood with agreement with money. He drank the lemon juice with the blood saying a prayer.

"Dear Lord, show in this devil, Lucifer invested toxic the truth of your power to stop an evil joy in life in Jesus Christ amen." Dewey came to the news someone sued the club and shut the business down by one receiving AIDS at the ranch club. Dewey remembers the women by seeing the pattern of the television news by its possession being the same as the stories in the television show and he senses once no stop to this nonsense on what he was connecting in seeing, but his awe in having an ability no one has is his drive to be the one to give the power in life to stop the evil routine.

He always remembers the black-haired women by the blood taste of each one and how they matched the look of the sexy witches in the horror stories. He smiles at the memory, knowing he did not get AIDS from them by being protected by the Lord. He also stares at the memory of him holding his father's gun shooting his momma in the head for raping him as he gets into watching the television. Seeing death is the stop of the act in being nature evil wrong. Dewey grew seeing the sight of God killing his abusive father knowing a plaque teaches one to stray from God's actual commands. Dewey's first time in the law was forgiven by the state and he received probation as their forgiveness of a high-class felony crime.

Dewey eyes the TV in awe knowing forgiven strikes the happy of Dewey. He forgives the writers and the maker of the TV structure and how one care is hard to art in this way of the world of TV and with its news, he wonders how one can care and not be bland? So far, he sees forgiveness and death for this, as his two parents died and the government forgiving him having him have a second chance in life. Dewey truly faiths one day no harm will be done to another. Dewey's cell phone rings.

"Hello, it's Icy, got a job, mean my two guys got a job, sounds easy steady, it's a temp service dealing with grounds maintenance type of work. Them able to keep up."

"Good, good, they're able to keep up for months. We are good to go."

"Yes, Dewey, they will." Dewey says his next move for Icy and ends the call. Dewey goes back to staring and watching the TV with its programs in the new millennium from having a usual note of a Lucifer-like character from growing up in the seventies with the abuse being the main roll in Dewey finding God in what he sees and experiences with paved justice to he before the age of twenty. His mom dead at age eight and death of his father at age seventeen. Since then, Dewey has been on his own with the help from the government at times in growing things his ability in wisdom with his way of the Lord hating the devil. Lucifer at seeing his whisper firsthand in his life.

"Don't do that I spark up memory of your mom raping you," is the whisper he heard and use too while he focused his energy in killing the devil by doing workouts, then later eating, and sexual ejaculation mostly by masturbating with including the acts he does in life helping another out with his ability. Dewey growth bravery determined strength in what he is doing can do so with proper guidance in his life by listening to God's empowering voice within him. He made a structure 3'6'9', soul meets flesh then meets spirit in the form given in the holy bible by God breathing a soul into man in his flesh made by he: God and later learn spirit is with him with while living flesh and soul. We have three parts to ourselves Dewey learns and made a system with the concept of three parts tying with God's word, his lesson.

Three equals one with the Lord by the three—flesh soul and spirit, six equals full circle all life comes to full circle and nine equals death to evil in the universe a clean end. He uses the three-part system in exercise in his everyday doing like walking and breathing. His muscle of prayer is able to stop one being a witch, stop one committing a crime, nor a sin is Dewey's goal in life in glorifying his flesh with soul in the grace to God and from his spirit that is with God and set to see it in the everyday news. Guilt comes in his life seeing court TV from thinking about his case. He paid his debts to society and makes sure he does not do it again. He has a plan in the relationship of sexual is have one last girlfriend and make it best, so far, he enjoys knowing more that.

Tim is unlocked and has the ability to absorb a function of what Dewey has been sighting out to him. It gives Dewey closure on having a girlfriend receiving this information about him. In lust eye, he likes black-haired women. Dewey now sits more back watching the action-packed TV show as it shows black-haired women. Dewey puts two and two together and has a fantasy of his chosen one will be black-haired as Karen. Dewey has always set his sights on Karen. Dewey sits now more relaxed back in the lofty light chair into watching the action-packed TV show in humbling thoughts of Icy's men got jobs and the start of the plan to end Richard Green's life is beginning with.

Now Dewey has to wait a good amount of months to have the men be stable at their jobs to have a story in just in case one tracks down Dewey and asks why his men are renting the room at this hotel known for its casino chain. Plus Dewey built a gaming persona on winning the games and by the winnings with the story of having a job with his brother whom is Tim as well having a steady paying job and here for a two years or more for his job. Dewey has that for Tim on his account at the hotel. Dewey and Tim have been good for the long rent at the hotel.

Dewey's main worry is his four-man crew he is using in life for his acts with the stress to ease off. He digs more into action TV shows with giggling showing adrenaline with his reasons why he watches the TV shows in know of his ability. Tim went to rest knowing he will go with Dewey to gamble later while the notice for a job is for closer up contact somehow to Richard Green as he is being Dewey's best friend enjoying his time unlocking a mystic ability learning from Dewey.

October 22, 2014

Dewey is fifty-one years of age. It's been seven months at the Missouri luxury casino hotel in Saint Louis. Since then Tim got a stable job part-time job being a janitor for a grocery store four miles in the city. Dewey in happiness in set calm doing his plan, working and having the story for the individuals who are tracking Richard Green going an hour away from the city from all four points to find him. Soon Dewey's going to make the offspring of Lucifer main element being used to destroy humanity in Dewey's mind to confess.

With this confession, the offspring will bring to light to Dewey on how to kill Richard Green. With James Taylor being on Dewey's thoughts, the young guy that works for Green and finding them both as well. Dewey learns to deal with the emotions of killing this man by watching the world as a whole with its news and seeing live events taking place everywhere. Humanity is being hurt by our own selves and he sees these two men being Lucifer being the master of giving pain for a better life dwelt against the Lord God.

Dewey grins, noticing Richard Green in his thoughts while playing Texas hold 'em with a young thirty-four-year-old male with buzz-cut hairstyle. James Taylor holding $80,000 pocket wearing diamonds in his glasses, sporting a dark causal blue pants and white T-shirt with blue strips. Dewey wins the hand. Dewey smiles knowing the offspring of Lucifer is confessing by having him win the hand, being used to help one life from evil connect living in rich from its doing and have it corrected stable living with having an immortal sense as it has been in Dewey's attention with Dewey having it made to be the other way around instead for evil for him the immortality.

He sought this sight out of immortality in receiving message with having messages sent to him by a world head living in the United States of America, noticing Dewey and knowing his reasons of actions grown to Dewey from this foul play as a rebel, infusion of their wealth welt weight of living. Richard Green is another confession by the offspring in Dewey's dreams in sleep. And sometimes when Dewey was alone, he saw this dude in a dream state while awake, a hardened vision seeing Richard Green's olive skin, blackened hair, and toned, middle-age build with flashy suits on during this vision states.

The offspring had Dewey do an online look on Richard Green in his forties by making him see him and by hearing his name in whispers during the vision dreamlike state and the search came heavier in porn. When asked about in the jungle of hardened thirst for the money, he came more heavier in sex trade in closed doors for decades. Dewey then knows about the operations by buying the women online posts from the online company that is made and founded by Richard Green. With him buying the women he had the offspring confess in their takes about Richard Green, his main play is supplying the captured a wealthy lifestyle for them not knowledgably getting raped into paradise.

Dewey came to set his direction in life in killing Richard Green and anybody involved. Dewey had learned to live with the offspring of Lucifer by it being a traitor to its nature. Dewey had killed it having clean breathe in air to grasp in confession with it witness as it happens every time Dewey prays since then. In silent motion with his eyes closed, and he got that muscle stronger over the years. Dewey enjoys his ability in highest awe in quiet by the main form of his ability comes from the hurt from being abused and raped, clash with anger in being released in acts that stops the pathways of rutted evil. Dewey's favorite is giving the people, strangers money in a sense of helping them out of a rut. Also, he enjoys the ability in giving him the sense to spot out a wicked person.

He likes to chew the toothpick in faith by having the needy get more money in receiving it and the wicked get the Lord directly in life by his chews in faith. He learns to do the faith by being on the wrong side of the law before he was twenty. A Lord directed in seeing life as it is with correct path to the stable life of mystic in natural sense with its glow of supernatural to ones know and the ability to sight the sought out to explain the ability of the Lord. Dewey in journey of depths of evil when the nature is enjoyed to kept living and have its headline shine in laughter of the whisper of Lucifer being tied to a human in Dewey's record of whom been noticing him.

Yet Dewey has no true sighting of the person that helps Lucifer best to be made given life in god's world. Showing its ability by the news and the stories being told with written plays of old delight path to movies that shape a face of evil in its theater with matching the news that partake during the TV's day and night life, a hyper fashion from the newspaper the TV news is. Dewey still stays determine he will meet the one that consumes this energy with all the satisfaction in life from its evil doings.

Dewey chews his toothpick in more serious as he raises the bet on double kings in his hand. The young man that works for Richard Green calls. Three cards show on the light blue carpet table. A seven of hearts, jack of spades and ten of diamonds. Dewey smiles and bets all in. The young man figs a little, yet still overconfident about his triple tens. He too goes all in with Dewey. Both players cards show. Double kings on the left and double tens matching third ten in pocket on the right. Dealer shows the fourth card is five of diamonds. The dealer then draws the last card, comes to be a king of hearts. Dewey wins all James Taylor money. The worker for Richard Green enjoys coming to this casino got tempered.

Dewey likes Texas hold 'em and glad's this guy's favorite game is Texas hold 'em. Dewey grins that he gotten a win over him. Dewey leaves the table with being confirmed he gotten what he needed by playing with him, he will go back to the room and channel in all the offspring ability about this young man that works for Richard Green, especially by the chips he touched and was holding. Dewey holds the chips in a small cart with touching them with his right hand as he walks back to his room. Dewey is back in the room as Tim leaves to go gamble practicing his mystic after seeing Dewey in the room with the chips. Dewey sits on the standard hotel room chair and holds the chip that was in James Taylor's hand all the time during the match. "Confess the whereabouts of the man gives evil its wealth from his pawn that held this chip in Jesus Christ name amen." Dewey has his eyes closed while said this prayer and flashes as lightening came in his see with a cold breeze form in air while his eyes are closed then visions of seeing Richard Green from James Taylor's point of view, Dewey begins seeing.

He sees a contract in Richard Greens hand while a trailer is filled with teenage boys made to be she males in the porn industry by the alertness of the mind know consciousness of James thinking it while James closes the door to the trailer, Richard Green signs the paper. He squeezes his eyes more having the offspring of evil confess something that is worthy to use for Dewey to get close to him. Dewey then at awe seeing his house around Saint Louis, Missouri. He sees the young man, James knocking on the door of the house, seeing a frame of his house, seeing visions of parties and meetings. Dewey opens his eyes and says, "His home, his beauty home is the spot. Yes, the core energy where he sleeps. an object of sort. This young man too." Everything about this James Taylor having the evil sense came true to Dewey, as Dewey holds the chip in his right hand.

Dewey puts the train of thought about Richard Green together seeing he is a CEO of a porn company and has wads of it in safe boxes and he one man that holds the kidnapping from poverty countries of the humans that brought in the sex trade, ones for breeding, to have one stable seeing it okay with knowing the norm is their best growth for the money, by keeping documents of legal contracts, and them don't give hassle at all when they become clit in the consciousness in the richen stable wealth lifestyle. Wives they become in train atmosphere and the usual become a sex object for money for life byb these guys with Richard Green. Dewey seeing and giggling while the chip is in his right hand still eyes open this time. "Death is the answer to you, since I saw you by this offspring, death has a festival and you need to ride the death mate, Green." Dewey puts the chip in the small black cart with the others and heads out of the room and goes to the cash out counter.

It is close to midnight on October 27, 2014, Dewey had the young thirty-four-year-old James Taylor followed by Icy and his men. Dewey is in the living room of James Taylor's home getting his account information while he is not home. Dewey's for certain he will not be at his home, so he broke a window to his house to get in. Once Dewey gets his account information, he going to wipe his account clean, also put it in the letter Dewey is making to give to a detective by mail as he did for the last act, giving worthful money to the public own by the freedom evils under the democrat party. A letter was sent with proof of worth to a detective of the state of New jersey and federal government about the high classed rich scene having evil demands being in power, there saving money that is worth billions has been given to the local people of New jersey state in the city by it's worth made given by a stranger whom is Dewey with details in the envelope stating the hundred dollars is worth more for being the made of it in early twentieth century and the acts of unlawful men with given proof.

Dewey has details of this letter to be given to the detectives with ID of this young man working for Richard Green and Richard Green's MO been detailed in the letter with documents of the handling exchange of the young teen children being put to submission in the given life by Green's supreme workers that makes them young teens into star fashion porn stars for the richen money and the sexual paradise of pigged men. Dewey searching through the

34 years old computer in the fifteen-foot living room for any information. Dewey's been at this for an hour and receive safe combinations in the drawers that has a gun in everyone. Dewey found the ones that has money and grab the stacks of the money in every safe.

He is holding a white clothed bag filled with the money and contracts that are in a yellow and brown envelope making proof of this guy's sex trade whereabouts. Dewey finally cracks the password having the offspring confess in the computer making the pass entry code for his files appear in complete without typing the password in the tab. His account number and what bank has what saved in the safe boxes came up and other accounts that has money in them shows up as Dewey prints out the paper with reading on.

"The imprint, the business company with the pictures of Green smiling with captured teens roped in the trailer pictured with him as the company name is on the trailer. You will be dead as Richard Green when this letter shows up to the detectives," Dewey said as he leaves the house with the paper having all this young man information including his social security number with the money from the safe boxes and the bank accounts info.

With what Dewey grab, he got Richard Green's address to go and grabbed a needing; a core object from James Taylor's life with the actions he does getting an object that means much to he is the connect heart thumping touch for Dewey set to kill he as he has his mind set to find one for Richard Green, as he has one for the young man he was gambling against at the casino. Dewey won the gambling match and now has his info to wipe his account clean, 10.3 million dollars all from the evil sex trade with legal contracts that bides Green to do illegal acts to get that pot for his worker.

Dewey gives the paper with the info to Tim. Tim already has the laptop ready before Dewey gotten back to the room to close this dude accounts.

Dewey then has a blue cloth, a huipil, the meaning object to James's life. Dewey found out by the offspring confess this time by scent, Dewey smelt a strong scent. Dewey followed the strong scent smell of a women body and found the huipil before he left the house after he gotten the information of his money accounts. As the offspring is tied with Dewey as his mystic ability, Dewey has not fully prayed the offspring away for it shows its use for the good as Dewey uses it for his benefit in learned rebel as he sees himself. Dewey grabs the blue clothe, sets it in a turtle shell on the table in the right corner of the hotel room. He pours small amount of gasoline on it from a small lighter fluid can.

He lights it with a match as he prays: "Dear Lord the wicked works of this man is forgiven and the court has judge he to end his life for thus he uses his life for evil wicked in immoral sexual paradise and will naught turn his head away enjoying the spoils of it, I pray death to this man in Jesus Christ existence amen," Dewey said as in praying then giggles as he sees the blue huipil burn in the turtle shell. He is giggling loud and long with his pure reason to end the regular routine of evil with knowing Icy informed he had to go to the hospital for coughing up blood and Tim stops his actions looks at Dewey at awe in the morning at the casino hotel in Saint Louis, Missouri.

Tim has been working on his way of the ability and the notice of Dewey every time makes the ability work. Tim must think of Dewey for it to work every time he uses it. Tim noted this and means to say something about it to Dewey, but he is enjoying seeing another plan of an act perform as Dewey giggles on the other side of the white walled hotel room. November 6, 2014, Its the next month, Dewey found out Richard enjoys staying at home in the fall. He has only a small open window to gather what he needs for his plan and finds comfort that he enjoys staying home which means there is an object he is close too. Dewey is in Green's business room inside his six-arc property home.

"Confess in heat burning the whereabouts of this man Richard Greens currency," Dewey commands and begins to feel heat coming from a safe box underneath the computer desk. He grabs it puts it on the desk, lightly touch the box feeling the heat. The roll numbers of the combination lock put in to place as Dewey touches the box to be ready open. Dewey opens the silver box as the heat wares away, he finds a sheet of paper with account numbers, a floppy disk, and a USB drive port along with fifty thousand dollars. He grabs them in excitement with little giggling. He slightly reads the sheet, he sees the routing numbers of accounts for bank, plus their account numbers, as the sheet is alike a bank statement. He folds it away to his pants pocket and puts the others in the white cloth bag.

"As you confess, now show the thing with the heart attachment that would bring death to this evil man in ceremony of prayer purpose of ending the life of evil rutted," Dewey commands the offspring of Lucifer again. Dewey then hears glass breaking. He leaves the room and follows the sound. He knows one is in the house by spying on Richard Green for the past week, When Richard left an hour ago, Dewey broke a window to one of his bedrooms of Richard Green's two-arc house upon the 6-arc land. The broken glass sound reminds Dewey he has to go out the same window. Dewey walks around the living room end up seeing a picture frame broken on a black steeled shelf having a glass for a base to stand things on. He grabs it sees two people in picture, one is Richard Green and the other a young female at age about nineteen.

"Certain this is it," Dewey says as he takes the picture out of the frame and puts in his white cloth bag. Dewey now begins to exit out the house from the bedroom window. Dewey walks out the window and heads to another white Camaro that he bought here in Missouri while icy and his men were tracking Richard down without Dewey making the offspring confess, that is parked on the south side of the six-arc land filled with wild trees and plants aside the two-arc wooden house. Dewey starts the engine with comfort that he gotten the right things to dwell his plan to end this dude's life as he knows it. He drives knowing Richard Green is responsible for most of the sex trade in the United States of America with having a flamboyant lifestyle, selling off teenagers and having a based business of it.

He grabs his white bag with his right hand, opens the bag to find the picture that was in the broken frame as he prayed in demand to get an object that is close to Richard Green to pray death in earliest form to be. He holds the picture at the steering wheel studying it. Drives on the highway back to the hotel. He then flips the picture, sees white blank and the word labeled Daughter '88. Dewey puts the car in cruise control. Breathing four long separate breathes. Seeing his momma touching him in a flash. Having himself look as son from the daughter word. He squeezes his arm muscles and breathes.

"Daughter? Out of what you do, your daughter is the symbol of your life? The most imagine. Of course, the usual thought, your daughter isn't fucked in the head with knowing what you actual do Richard," Dewey said alone staring at the picture driving back to the hotel then giggles and says, "Don't worry you will be dead evil produce, those teens don't need sex, they need a home." Dewey arrives at the hotel daybreak later. He was driving all night from Richard Green's place west from Saint Louis, Missouri. The picture of Richard Green and his daughter is in the turtle shell. Dewey is rolling up a cigarette and going to smoke and stare at the picture more with awe relaxed knowing this act is real. He is going to pray as before. The young guy James Taylor and now James's boss Richard Green. Their accounts wipe clean, and the money is in Dewey's account.

Soon as Dewey walks in the room, he gave the info to Tim to gather the money from Richard's account with James Taylor account to another account then to Dewey's account where it is untouchable. He has his offspring of Lucifer with Lucifer's host somewhere in the united states of America be the confession, the energy ability for the offspring to help Dewey by completing any task at an atm nor a bank teller, for both uses the computer. The offspring uses itself, Its own existence to have Dewey pass all obstacles meaning when Dewey goes to get money, he gets it. There is no block towards him, no way to court him in law about the money, and if trouble comes the account will disappear along with its money. Dewey inhales the smoke enjoying the satisfaction has with his ability. He exhales the smoke with joy staring at the picture in gloat knowing this two guys life will end soon and it puts an imprint stop to their natural course of their evil lives and the people around them that are involve with the evil rotten sex trade. Dewey ends the cigarette and walks to the turtle shell on the wooden table in the right corner of the hotel room near the second bed. Pours the lighter fluid on the picture.

He then lights it on fire with a match praying, "Dear Lord, the person I bring in henceforth to early death is a person consume in adultery, depths to get there in immorality paradise he is part of the core, I pray to end this person's life and forgive his actions clean in the form given and showed me by touching the heart, the closeness of this person reason living and in given vision of showed unchanged habit with its unlearned heart to stop the evil in the frame of this person life living, I pray this justice will live in death in he as in breath in Jesus Christ name amen." Dewey looks on at the burning picture having a white circle painted around the turtle shell on a gray sheet of paper with the holy bible nearby glaring in shine. Tim walks towards Dewey as Dewey stares at the picture in the turtle shell.

"It's been a year and a half we have been here. We got the money and now just six more days and I will trail them two," Tim says to Dewey.

"The deaths of them two will great our rebel cause as we growth it, my friend. The end of evil and it is form of growth. Guilt is my shine in forgiveness, the awe in return is not to fuck it up. Them both deaths will complete more awe, my friend."

"Yes, indeed, bro. In God we trust," Tim responds to Dewey.

November 8, 2014

"Yes, the money's secured and there is no need no more."

"You sure Dewey, no more."

"Yes, Icy, no more."

"You showed the weight, you good, Dewey, ever in need come find me, Dewey, take care honestly."

"Bye, man." Dewey let Icy end the call as he is slightly giggling in knowing Icy and his men got sickness. They are slowly dying early in their lives. Dewey is waiting for Tim to come in the room with the news on Richard Green and James Taylor. Tim and

Dewey both just only used the cell phone for an act for Icy. Dewey and Tim have a special connection. They contact each other by being on time and keeping their word. Dewey and Tim build that connection and Dewey grows his consciousness-aware muscle in using that energy for him with Tim being another person extra load of energy along now to end the evil. The continued rut in life that harms humanity in silent growth.

Guilt and forgiveness come from Dewey's true heart in one act he did at the age of nineteen. He had a couple raped to death by a demon, the offspring Dewey came to learn to live with in life that is loyal to him. The couple was walking out of the convenience store, going to their car and spotted Dewey and made fun of him. Dewey's reaction was anger and the demon felt it with him, the demon made the couple see itself as it heightens their sexual organs in pain while giving them both a heart attack. Dewey was young and had the mood no one is allowed to hurt me no more. The offspring felt this at his age and went hyperactive. Later positive coaching came to Dewey from that murder, being raped to death by a demon and only Dewey knows what was happening to them when they were screaming seeing in depths the offspring of Lucifer giving them painful sexual act to death.

Dewey lives his life directing his attention to the one that whispers to him in paranormal state of being in his choice with the Lord. He stares at the table with the clean turtle shell still on the table and does his best to cry the guilt out as the natural process, but he knows thinking of what makes him feel somewhat guilty is the knowledge of what is needed of going is justified manner to growth himself with his ability a human heart more as his routine exercise. Tim comes in the room and Dewey just swallows the feeling of guilt and corrects his voice box.

"Whoa, the two are dead by a heart attack, Dewey. What you did in not needing me, man, was just and nice. The end of evil, Dewey, you are it. The complete structure in not needing evil twine in life of we, you are that imprint."

"Good, only you know, friend. WE are it, you agreed on being here with me, so it is we are the imprint."

"Yeah, man, an ambulance showed at them two houses and could not stop the heart attack, man. One was with a wife, the other a usual work gal from their business."

"Nice, an imprint from nowhere and a letter showing up to the detectives, hopefully work will be done in our faith, friend."

"Yeah, man. I'm working in thought to give money out too, man. You got me going, man. Wait till I see my girl back in Jersey. If she's still available."

"Right, man, we leave later tonight," Dewey responds to Tim as he stares at the turtle shell trying to cry out guilt as an exercise process. Dewey's last learn step is to channel the offspring to the ones that have been trailing Dewey all his life, having an Indian show up at the times of these events in Dewey's life. Now Dewey's expecting someone to show up to Dewey and say something that no one else would know. He just hopes it would be in front of Tim when it happens so someone would believe him, and he would like it to be Tim too.

Dewey stares at the cherry of his cigarette and begins to hear, gasoline is your memories, I hate your gasoline. The flame cherry then burns out in mid-range. Dewey minds himself in awe seeing what he explained to his ole lady Karen how an enemy is paranormal form being existing to him since childhood and as a huge title being known as Lucifer. He shown his ability to Karen, by the offspring being a traitor to its nature having a connect to

Dewey as its personality growth itself to him with Dewey being his life reason to be the one to stop the currently evil that takes place in this world. Karen reacted in slightly excited awe with laughter of happiness on how he able to get cash and the needs to get by surviving life by the offspring tide itself to Dewey knowing Dewey had killed it, it awes Dewey.

Since then it came back alive by Dewey's command. A living suicide in happiness comfort towards Dewey the offspring has from Lucifer the evil entity along with Dewey. Lucifer the being hates this feeling it offspring has for Dewey, the comfort from its tail touch by its offspring being a hypocrite, it does best to strike Dewey down. Dewey relights the cigarette after doing four breathes to ease his mood knowing this is still new to him. This war his energy being a light to the stable darkness that lives among the world has the life of self-struggle, Dewey feels like he can break anytime, seeing himself walking down a grocery aisle lashing out pointing the point his parents never cared for him justifying his actions and be a thriller to another person, instead he does his homework lash out in righteous against the wicked to imprint the stop of the movement of an evil route that is tied to a current of everyday hurt to humanity.

He breathes on smoking the cigarette in high alert this war is new. The meetings of the people tide to this entity Lucifer and how they truly don't know the ability he has is based on knowledge he read and live with in natural experience with able to destroy another life, yet Dewey attentions his determined strength in life to a picture of one home having Christmas without any drama and hurt, without any ways of abuse to destroy the home family loved feeling that meant to happen for a family at Christmas instead having a shitty Christmas year after year without family. In this kept vision he directs his self to a maturity in everyday of his life after his drama before the age of twenty more. He breathes the tobacco in faith of all humanity having no way of getting hurt from the time they awake to sleep. Slowly he breathes more resting on the edge of his bed in the apartment house he is renting in the city of the state New Jersey.

He breathes consuming what he did and does on the regular, being a help to end evil nature. Smoke out of his mouth he thinks of walking out of the house going to the homeless and give his free money that he gets by his ability to them. He inhales the menthol smoke knowing death is his friend, "I continue my smoke, I have not given up. Whisper to me, I am just a thought away to stop another routine of yours, sure your offspring enjoys death," Dewey whispers in strength as he exhales the smoke and putting the lighter back on the small table in front of him near the TV. He continues to smoke in his purpose of praying with a grin on his entire face from his ole lady Karen.

He looks at her with awe as she is sleeping next to him on his right. She is naked under the covers filled with joy in sleeping. Dewey gives her money in chime of loving her. Dewey as well comforts her, joyous to her needs. Dewey aims Karen to be his last try at love. Again, he stares at the cherry of the cigarette seeing his memories, seeing Richard Green not living. Been a year since he went to Missouri. He sees the young man not living in abuse of life filled with bad sex. He stares at the cherry seeing those items burn in the turtle shell with his burning passion to have the nature of toxic corruption end; to have one life not in trauma harm. He turns back center flicks the chunk of ash to a red ashtray as its shows the symbol of money the wealth burned. He puts his energy in smoking, he grew up where smoking was everybody's habit and tend to make beneficial use of smoking, so he tides it a prayer of faith relief satisfaction. Dewey finishes the cigarette in thinking of his memories remembering what the whisper said then goes to bed.

It is fall October 12, 2015; Dewey is fifty-two years old living with his girlfriend Karen. He is planning another act to do and have more stability growth in what he been doing at the age he is, putting imprints of stop to evil routines in everyday life by prayer with excess acts. He uses his love for Karen and the time spent with her in energy for the prayer to stay virgins until merry in Jesus Christ name amen. Dewey form that prayer act by dreaming what he would do when he gets a girlfriend. He asks what prayer the core time be spent with his chosen: to arouse meaning shocking sparks of his time living with his ability having prayer, a connect with God to enhance his life in happiness. Karen agrees with using her love in living the prayer as well with her noticing Dewey more with his ability this time around.

Dewey always made sure Karen is his paradise meet. Dewey more in happiness this time with planning to put a stop to another evil routine by being with Karen. It is seven p.m. Dewey drinking tea with honey with Karen at a coffee shop. The fall wind breezes through the open windows at the shop. He enjoys evening spent with Karen, having someone there in an instant with building a relationship in closeness. "I am not looking to exceed my bloodline and I acknowledge our age number; I am glad you are here with me Karen. The gloss of our days shines with our work in loving each other, I love you, Karen."

"I love you too, Dewey," Karen says in trust knowing Dewey means honestly worded heart. The first time they kissed Karen felt at home with Dewey and Dewey did not taunt for sex.

"In what I do, I put stops in routines of immoral behavior. What I show is the choice the people make; it is based off their energy with touched by mine. My energy is equipped in ending the natural evil we tend to see in regular process as the news. What I'm telling you is I am leaving for a while, but I will be in touch, and will you be okay with that?" Dewey then spits it out at the end asking her will she accept being with Dewey as he leaves.

"It is what you do, Dewey. When are you leaving? And yes, I will be in touch with you, I am okay in what you do and have, Dewey, you talk as harm should never come between us."

"Just do not know right now, looking doing homework, but I had to ask just in case I leave earlier like a couple of months. You can still stay at the apartment for long as you want."

"Alright, I was thinking like a week or soon you will be leaving," Karen said.

"Yeah, not early, got to fill my satisfaction and my satisfaction is being with you, Karen."

"Glad to know, Dewey" Karen responds while drinking her tea in smiles.

The next afternoon Dewey is on his laptop looking up the man Max Lowe. He is one head responsible for sex trafficking in the south of the United States of America. Dewey is determined to find anything on him. Karen is relaxing in a chair chatting on the phone with her dad her only parent living as Dewey sits on the couch with the laptop in the living room of the apartment Dewey is staying in with Karen making his mark in happiness in what he does. Dewey can easily put a face to Max Lowe, hazel eyes matching his blonde hair with the length touching his jawbone line and tan skin with his 6-foot structure is noticeable in a crowd.

He has not yet have his address right now and he is bested

to find it. Dewey then chews on a toothpick, thinking and staring at Karen and in a slight touch to the toothpick by his right thumb and index finger he demands, "Confess." He chews the toothpick more doing his best to make the offspring confess: to show it works about Max Lowe. The screen of the laptop then shows a website address to Max Lowe home address in a flash. Dewey smiles then clicks on the address among other links below. A page on the website for searchone.com appears having the latest picture of Max Lowe along with his current address and a file tab to see his criminal background and his background in general. Dewey reads the page, click on the tabs, and gets Max Lowe current address. He stares at Max Lowe's picture that is loaded up on the screen. Dewey remembers meeting Max once in Nevada at a porn expo. Dewey went there for homework; he had a guy name Ron tell him about Max Lowe at the expo. Dewey just introduced himself to Max there as a fan for porn, but Dewey has his eyes set on killing anyone who produced rape.

He got talking to Ron, then set his eyes on Max Lowe, a terrible sex trafficking he does in the south country in the United States of America. Ron told Dewey everything about Max Lowe and his operations by being attached to the offspring of Lucifer, Dewey used his ability to get the information he needed about going to the expo in 2011. Dewey stares at Max picture hard, knowing Max's fame is not with the crowd with porn, his fame is in the crowd of the hardcore wicked who buys from Max Lowe, seeing Max's handsomeness that consumes friendly talk that makes you not shy to say hi back to him when he would talk to you. Dewey in deep thought knowing what Max does to get that high class look and the lifestyle that leaves him not to cook his own plate. Dewey begins to feel pain as like you are being forced to do something feeling in being pain as he stares at Max's picture on the couch in his living room still.

"The wonder you will not stop doing what you do thrills me to end your rodeo living life," Dewey whispers. Dewey quickly thinks of a way of kill Max Lowe by channeling himself to Max by the offspring realizing Max is sold to the devil in life, hence the offspring host Lucifer and squeezes his fist with every righteous emotion playing it out to have Max drop dead as he squeezes his fist with the reasons in power mode being mystical to kill him. He thinks of ways to confront him to do so. Breathing heavy, Dewey closes his eyes, getting his composure opens his eyes and sees Max Lowe blonde hair on the screen and giggles.

December 8, 2015

Dewey stares at Max at a bar located in the southern part of Oklahoma state. Dewey spent three weeks with dried icy air weather on the address that was given to him and found Max Lowe on the second week as Max was coming out of his house in the morning going somewhere. Dewey found out he goes to an office building in the mornings. On weekends he goes to this bar. Dewey has been lucky because the word about Max is he travels a lot. Dewey catches on to Max's routine coming to this bar on Saturday nights. Dewey pays attention at Max's play, the office days, just moving a pen and speaking on the phone having some blockage way of his real job that he does sex trafficking.

Max is chatting on his phone sitting near the counter bar area by a window. Dewey has been sipping on beer, sitting four seats behind Max afar from the bar counter. All his emotions about a person not realizing to stop the evil act after knowledge of a one being sued for minors in porn is the focus in channeling the offspring of Lucifer from Max existence being claim to evil. Dewey feels heated, a little sweat breaking out as he is wearing a light gray zipped jacket. Dewey in thought of prayer, sees his mom, the person who would not stop raping him as he stares at Max, the singlet with mother's Dewey's was darkened it growth him to end the wicked steps that is destroying life.

Dewey is waiting for Max to go out of the bar to have a cigarette. It's been an hour and Max brings out his cigarette box while he is chatting still on the phone. Dewey quickly gets ready, waits for him to walk out while he is on his fifth beer, and he is stable drunk having the offspring heat him on standby. Dewey wipes off the little sweat with a napkin and sees Max walking out now with a cigarette in his mouth. He finishes his beer at a calm pace. Dewey then grabs his cigarette case out of his left pants pocket and walks out.

"Plenty, the load is the money," Max said on his cell phone, standing in the smoking area on the left coming out from the bar. Dewey walks and bumps into him. They stand face-to-face.

"Sorry," Dewey says in contact with Max and Max is full eyes on Dewey, then falls down to the ground…unmoving. Max is dead on the cold ground. No one else is around Dewey and Max. Dewey's sweating begins to stop and he walks off east towards to his hotel room.

December 10, 2015

It's been two days since the Max encounter and his death. Dewey is in smiles, giggling and knowing the minors and anybody helpless won't be trafficked and the headache towards the evil routine sets in after Richard Green, James Taylor, and now Max Lowe, three major persons for the sex trafficking dead, unable to call a shot nor make a move. Dewey is lying on his hotel white sheeted bed living out his last week in the hotel in Muskogee, Oklahoma five miles from the bar where he killed Max by using his mystical ability. Someone knocks on the door. Dewey struggles to the thought to open the door a little while calming down; then he gets his posture to open the door.

"Rebel fat boy, remember me!" Dewey's door has no peephole to see who is on the other side of the door. Dewey hears those words as he falls to the ground being tasered, yet no electric machine is hooked up to Dewey. Dewey then begins to shake quickly, and he sees only two hands having the fingers at point with pressure as in pushing on a wall. Dewey still shaking looks up and sees in a blur a black-haired, dark-red tanned individual and remembers him trailing him all his life. Dewey struggles in breathing having Karen in vision in flashes with Dewey's full body, then unable to move like being shell shocked. The long, black-haired dark-reddish tanned man in late middle age having gray whiskers steps over Dewey and Dewey hears the man's heartbeat overlapping his with being frozen and the man closes Dewey's eyelids with both hands as Dewey then dies during that motion. Dewey had Karen in his thoughts and heard the words, "Mess with the reign well, fat boy, time to end the rebel with a cause."

– Lollipop, the shape of the moving shake in the dance, the crack see as hallucination never leaves and one left to have not say it, never left kid. The past was always looney crazy insane. I leave to you as that in knowing you enjoyed my holiness in leaving as that – Dewey